A Summer Day in the Park

The cicadas are finally buzzing again. Lately, there has been a lot of rain.

The air was cold and wet, and the cicadas were quiet. It did not feel like summer.

But today the cicadas are buzzing. I close my eyes and listen to them humming. They make the sound, *Zaa, zaa, zaaa!*

A soft, warm breeze brushes my cheek. It only just stopped raining, so the summer heat has not come back yet.

"It's going to be sunny all day!" Ben announces, walking onto the porch. He has two giant glasses of iced tea and a bright smile on his face. "Mom, do you want sugar?"

"Not too much," I say. Ben hands me the glass in his right hand. I sip the tea. It's cool, tangy, and just a little sweet. "Perfect!" I sigh. A mockingbird flies by, trilling a happy tune.

The sweat from my cold glass trickles down my wrist.

"Do you still want to go to the park today?" Ben asks me.

I look up at the deep blue sky and its piling, soft summer clouds. "If it's going to be sunny all day, yes!" I say. "Let's go right now!"

We finish our tea. Then I go back inside to change. I wear my favorite lavender blouse. Its fabric is soft and cool. Should I wear a skirt or some pants? I choose the skirt, even though we might sit in the grass. The skirt is long and white. It makes me feel like a bride or a princess.

Of course, I must bring my hat. The sun looks bright today after so much rain. I'm so excited to spend time in the park! It felt like the rainy days would never end.

"You look wonderful, Mom!" Ben says when I step outside.

He helps me into the car. We drive to his house first. Ben says that Hannah wants to come too. Of course she does. My granddaughter loves the outdoors even more than I do.

"Should we buy her some treats?" I ask Ben.

He wrinkles his nose. "You're spoiling her, Mom!"

I smile. "That's what grandmas are for."

Ben sighs. "How about we all get something together, at the park?"

I like this idea. Maybe Hannah can show me her favorite ice cream stand. I settle back in the car seat and open my window. The wind buffets my cheek. It smells like freshly cut grass.

People outside are mowing their lawns. One man stops. Wiping sweat from his red, shiny face, he turns and waves at us.

It isn't a long ride to Ben's house. There is a dogwood tree in the front yard. Robins hop around on the ground nearby. Their breasts are rusted red. I smile when they cock beady black eyes at the car.

"They aren't flying away," I say.

"That's because my wife keeps feeding them bread crusts," Ben explains. "See how fat they are?"

I chuckle. The robins are a little plump. They hop closer to the car, chirping hopefully. I can see their soft feathers and downy throats that wobble as they sing. One looks down and snatches a wriggling worm. It still looks at me like it wants a bread crust.

"Ben," I say to my son, "when you fetch Hannah from the house, bring me some bread. I want to feed the birds at the park."

Ben nods. He leaves the air conditioning on and goes inside. I sit, caught between warm sunlight from the windows and cold air coming from the vents.

This car is still new. Its seats are soft and velvety.

The air still smells fresh and sweet, like a new car. My eyelids feel suddenly heavy. It's so warm and relaxing. I almost want to take a nap.

Suddenly, the car door opens. "Hi, Grandma!" Hanna squeals. She jumps into the car. Her small arms wrap around me tightly. I love hugs.

Giving her a squeeze, I say, "Hello, Hannah! Are you excited for the park?"

Hannah nods. Her hair is twisted into a pretty, brown braid. She's wearing a Disney princess t-shirt and shorts. "Daddy brought bread!" she announces. "He says we're getting ice cream at the park!"

I smile and tap her freckled nose. "That's right! It was my idea."

Hannah giggles and gives me another hug. Her giggle is the cutest thing on this earth. It sounds like music and happiness. Just hearing it makes me smile.

Ben makes sure Hannah has her seatbelt on. Then he begins to drive toward the park. Hannah and I play "I Spy" on the way.

"I spy…I spy…" Hannah looks through the window. Her cute little forehead wrinkles. "I spy…something *blue*!"

"Is it the sky?" I guess.

Hannah cackles. "Nope! Guess again!" She's bouncing up and down in her seat.

I look out the window again. Cornfields surround us on either side. Their stiff green stalks shift in the breeze. I can see golden heads of corn peeking out from a few. But there is nothing blue except for the sky.

"Is it a bird?" I guess again.

Hannah is turning red from all her giggling. "Nope!" she gasps. "Guess again!"

I look out the window again. There *is* a small pond on the right. But it is small and covered in fat lily pads. The pond is more green than blue.

I guess anyway. "Is it the pond?"

Hannah folds her arms and puffs her skinny chest out. "*Nooo!*" she howls.

"Hey!" Ben warns from the front. But I can see him smiling.

"Sorry," Hannah says. Her voice is now a whisper. She leans towards me, dimples forming around her smile. "Three strikes!" she whispers to me. "I win!!"

I shrug my shoulders. "I'm absolutely stumped. What did you spy with your little eye?"

Hannah pats the soft, velvety seat beside her. "I spied with my little eye…Daddy's car!"

Of course! Ben's car, the one we are sitting in, *is* blue. It is a very shiny blue, too. I think he bought it last month.

"That was not fair, young lady!" I scold Hannah. "I think I am going to have to…*tickle you*!"

Hannah screams with laughter as I tickle her little body. She wiggles and jumps. But I am a tickling expert. Soon, little Hannah is gasping and hiccupping. She keeps making little giggles whenever I catch her eye. It looks like she even cried a few laughter tears; her brown eyes are shiny and wet.

"We're here!" Ben says. Hannah and I unbuckle our seatbelts. We get out of the car. The summer air feels *much* hotter after being in the air conditioning.

Even in the shade of the oak trees, I feel sweat gather on my neck.

Ben whistles. "It's a scorcher! Hannah, can you help Grandma put on some sunscreen?"

Hannah slathers her small hands in thick, white sunscreen. I gasp when she puts it on my arms. It's so cold! I rub it into my skin and help Hannah with her sunscreen. Then we hold hands and walk into the park.

Because it is such a beautiful day, lots of families are here at the park. I smile at babies in their strollers as they pass. Some young people are jogging by themselves. They have headphones in their ears and dark sunglasses. It's like they live in their own world.

One young woman doesn't have headphones *or* sunglasses. She does have a dog.

"He's so cute!" Hannah coos. The woman kindly stops to let Hannah pet her dog. The dog is small and covered in curly fur. It is golden brown, with large soft eyes and a small wet nose. Hannah scratches its long, floppy ears. The dog licks her chin, which makes her scream. I pet the dog, too. Its body is so, *so* soft, and wriggles with excitement at my touch.

"Good boy!" I exclaim. The dog rolls over, spreading its paws for a belly rub. Hannah and I pat the little round belly. The dog's tail, hardly more than a stubby puff on its bottom, wags happily.

We say goodbye to the kind lady. Ben wants to take some pictures, so we walk down to the pond. White geese are floating near the pond's fountains. When I look into the water, I can see reddish goldfish swimming around. They kiss the water's surface with hungry, *o*-shaped mouths.

Ben asks a nice stranger to take our picture. He stands in the middle and puts a warm, strong arm around my shoulder. Hannah sits on his other shoulder. Soon she will be too big to do that! We smile wide for the camera. *Cheese!* The summer sun is so bright. I can feel my eyes squinting. I hope I didn't blink!

Ben shows me the picture on his camera's tiny screen. I can't see it very well. "I'll print it out large for you, Mom," Ben promises me. "But it looks good!"

"I didn't blink?" I ask nervously.

"Not at all." Ben squeezes my hand. "How about you feed the geese with Hannah while I get ice cream?"

I sit by the pond with Hannah. Together, we break the soft crusts into little pieces. "If the pieces are too big, the babies can't eat them," I explain.

Hannah grabs a handful of crumbs. Standing on her toes, she throws her gift. But a breeze catches the crumbs, and they land right in front of us! This makes the goldfish happy. They splash around, shiny bodies of red and gold and black.

Hannah gasps as the water spatters on her toes.

I show Hannah how to take little pinches of the breadcrumbs and toss them gently. Soon, the geese come swimming towards us. The grownup geese are graceful.

They dip their long, beautiful necks and nibble at the breadcrumbs. The goslings are different. Squawking, they wiggle their baby tails to swim faster. They bump into each other and gobble at the crumbs. Hannah giggles at them.

"They need to share!" she says.

Soon, Ben comes back with three ice cream cones. Hannah takes the chocolate and I take the strawberry. The soft-serve ice cream melts sweet and cold on my tongue.

Its strawberry tang and sweetness are perfect. I lick the ice cream quickly, but it's already melting! My fingers get sticky.

Ben hands me a napkin. "Start at the bottom of the ice cream, Mom," he suggests. I do, and the melting isn't a problem anymore.

Hannah offers me a taste of her chocolate ice cream. "I need to share, too!" she announces.

"Good girl," Ben says proudly. I lick the deep, rich chocolate. It tastes so good with the strawberry ice cream!

We throw away our trash and walk through the park. Soon I see a few hydrangea bushes. The large, round flower bunches are a gentle lilac color.

They have yellow in their middles and smell like sweet jasmine. I touch the delicate petals and sigh with joy.

Hannah finds a playground to play on. She giggles that musical giggle as Ben chases her down the slide. I sit on the park bench to watch them.

There's another hydrangea bush beside me. This one is blue and yellow. When I look closer, I see a snail inching its way along the underside of a leaf. I stare at its stretching, slimy neck. The shell is dirt brown with a pretty black spiral. The snail's eye stalks turn towards me.

It shrinks into its shell and falls off the leaf.

In the distance, I can hear music. A woman is singing and playing the guitar. "It sounds like there's a live performance," says Ben, walking towards me with Hannah. "Do you want to check it out?"

I love music. "Let's!" I say. We follow the sound through the green, warm park.

The dirt paths are still muddy from the rain, so we stay on the sidewalk. Hannah jumps in one puddle before Ben tells her to stop. She pouts, her lower lip quivering dangerously. I sneak her a chocolate Hershey's kiss I've been saving in my purse. Hannah perks up at once.

The center of the park has a large, grassy field and a pavilion.

The singer is standing in the pavilion.

She has a chestnut-colored guitar and long, red hair. Her fingers dance across the guitar strings. The song is mellow and sweet, like summer ice cream. When the woman sings, my heart feels warm.

"Dance with me!" Hannah begs. I smile and take her hands.

We twirl around until my billowy blouse and skirt puff up with air. Then we lie down in the grass. One green blade pokes me in the ear. I lie on my back with Hannah. Ben joins us, and we take each other's hands.

The sky above goes on forever and ever. I stare into the deep blue and try to count the white, puffy clouds. "What shapes do you see in the clouds?" I ask Ben and Hannah.

"A cat!" Hannah replies at once. "It's white and fluffy, and so, *so* cute!"

"I'm not getting you a cat," Ben sighs. Hannah pouts again.

"I see a giant tree," I say. "It's big and strong. The leaves are white and don't give us any shade." The clouds really do look like treetops today, all large and round. They float lazily across the summer-blue sky.

"I see Sarah," Ben says. I smile. Even in a beautiful park, my son thinks about his wife.

"When is Mom coming home from her trip?" Hannah asks.

"Tomorrow," Ben replies.

"Maybe we should surprise her with a welcome-home gift," I say.

"Like a kitten!" Hannah offers.

"Nope," says Ben.

I sit up. The grass smells like summer and sunshine, but my back is starting to hurt. "Sorry, Hannah. I was thinking of making your mom a cake."

Hannah sits up, too. She's already forgotten about the kitten. "That's a great idea! Let's make it together!"

We decide to make the cake instead of making lunch. That means we should eat out before going home. Ben remembers seeing food stalls near the ice cream stand.

We leave the musician, but first I leave a five-dollar bill in her basket. She smiles and bows to me. Her hair is so long and red. My hair used to be red when I was younger. Now it's more of a pale silver. I don't mind. Hannah says my hair is star colored.

The summer sunlight has erased the cooler air from this morning. We trudge through the grassy field, dripping with sweat. I sigh in relief when we reach the shade.

There are many oak and pine trees here. They're not as big as the tree I saw in the clouds, but they give a lot more relief from the sun.

The cicadas are louder now that we're under the trees. They buzz and hiss so loudly that I can't hear myself talking.

"Kitty!" Hannah shouts. I blink. One on of the park benches sits a cat. It blinks at Hannah with sleepy, green eyes.

"Yelling will scare the kitty," Ben warns. Hannah shuts her mouth. Slowly, she stretches out her hand.

"Here kitty, kitty, kitty!"

The cat blinks again. It doesn't move.

"Let me try," I say. When my husband was still here, we fed stray cats in our garden. I walk slowly and steadily towards the cat. I don't look it in the eye. My hand is palm-up and open.

Soon, a timid wet nose touches my outstretched finger. Hannah gasps in delight.

"It looks like she's friendly," I say. The cat lets me scratch its chin. Its fur is black with marbled orange. I pet its head gently. The cat jumps down and rubs against my leg. I can hear the soft rumble of its purr.

Ben takes pictures as I show Hannah how to pet the cat. It's clear that she wants to take it home, but Ben points to the collar on the cat's neck.

"I bet she belongs to this park," he says. "Look at how fat and happy this cat is. People are feeding her here. This is her home."

Hannah gives the cat one last pet and lets us drag her away. We find the food stalls. Ben and Hannah get hot dogs and Gatorade. I prefer the BLT sandwich.

At the picnic tables nearby, we dig in. My sandwich is delicious! I sigh as the sweet tomato and salty bacon melt in my mouth. The rye bread is coarse but filling.

It reminds me of the bread my mama used to bake so many years ago. I wipe my fingers on a napkin.

Ants are struggling to lift some breadcrumbs I left behind.

After we put on some more sunscreen, Ben announces it's time to head back to the car. Hannah tugs at my hand as we walk. She's starting to trail behind, her feet dragging on the sidewalk.

Ben and I exchange a look. Hannah probably needs a nap.

"Tell you what," I say. "Why don't we stop at the bakery and buy your mom a cake?"

Hannah lights up. "Can I pick the cake?"

"Of course, sweetie," says Ben. "Mom will be really happy."

We make it back to the car at a better pace. Hannah still looks sleepy, but she's excited about the cake. Her little legs bounce as she sits in the car.

"Does your mama like chocolate?" I ask. "Or is she more of a shortcake or pound cake lady?"

"Mom likes shortcake!" Hannah says. "I want her cake to have lots of icing too!"

When we arrive at the bakery, Hannah is the first one out of the car. She's already staring hungrily at the cakes in the window. I'm still full from my sandwich, but the cakes look so tasty that my stomach growls.

The bakery door opens with a tinkle. Cool, sweet-smelling air hits us.

I walk in and stare at the shelves of cakes and Danishes. Juicy red strawberries and other colorful fruits top the decadent sweets. Icings of all flavors are spread beautifully across the cakes with spiraling spots of whipped cream dotted about.

Hannah chooses a round strawberry shortcake. The baker offers a free message. We have him scrawl, *Welcome home, Mom!* in beautiful chocolate script. The cake is boxed and packed with ice. I buy myself a Danish for later. Apple is my favorite, but the peach is seasonal. I decide to take the peach.

"Good choice," the baker says. "The peach Danishes are popular here!"

He winks at me, his eyes blue and twinkling over a bushy black moustache. I thank him and join Ben and Hannah in the car.

Now that she has her cake, Hannah falls asleep quickly on the ride home. Her head slumps against my arm, heavy and warm. I stroke her braided hair softly. Soon, she's snoring.

"We really wore her out," Ben comments with a smile.

"I'll need a nap myself after you take me home," I answer with a yawn. It's almost four p.m. The blazing summer sun is dipping behind the clouds. It looks like it might rain again.

"Should I drop you off first?" Ben asks me.

"Yes, please."

We pull into my driveway. My small garden looks a bit parched. Maybe I'll do some watering before dinner. Then again, I'm very tired. I yawn again.

"Will you be alright making dinner by yourself?" Ben asks. I smile at him.

"Don't you worry. I've got some leftovers in the fridge, and I just bought this tasty Danish. You take Hannah home and get that cake ready for Sarah."

"Okay, Mom. Just wanted to be sure." Ben looks at Hannah and chuckles. "She's fast asleep. I think there's a pillow under the seat."

There is a pillow. I tuck it gently under Hannah's head and pull away.

She shifts a bit in her sleep. After kissing her forehead, I get out of the car. Ben gives me a quick hug.

"Thank you for the wonderful day," I tell him.

"Anytime, Mom," he replies. "Let's go to the park again when Sarah comes back."

I watch the car as it pulls out of the driveway. The clouds are gathering. It will definitely rain. I don't need to water my garden tonight. I making my way inside to clean up a bit. The cicadas are still buzzing in the distance.

Their voices sound like, *Zaa, zaa, zaaaaa*. Their voices are quieter than before. Maybe like my granddaughter, they're tired after a long day.

I put my dinner in the microwave and wait on the porch. A soft, warm breeze brushes my cheek. It smells like a summer rainstorm: wet, grassy, and wild. The clouds are turning red in front of the setting sun.

The rain starts to fall as I eat my dinner. Drops pitter patter across my window. Thunder rumbles in the distance. I turn on the radio to hear the soft, drawling voice of a country singer. It reminds me of the red-haired woman in the park this afternoon. She had the sweetest smile. Maybe she's the one who feed the park bench cat. I hope the cat is staying dry in the rain.

Lightning flickers outside. I close the blinds.

After washing the dishes, I settle down in front of my television with the peach Danish and some ice cream.

There's a show on about a serious-looking detective. He's adjusting his bowler hat while a beautiful blond lady talks to him.

I take a bite of the Danish. The crust is flaky and tastes like butter. The peaches are perfectly soft and scrumptious.

My telephone rings. It's Ben.

"Hi, Mom. Check your e-mail. I sent you the pictures from today."

With Ben's help, I open my e-mail and look at the pictures. My favorite is the photo of all three of us.

We're standing in front of the pond. Hannah is clearly giggling as she sits on Ben's shoulder, her freckled face all scrunched up with glee. Ben has his arm around me, and he looks so much like his father with that handsome grin. I'm *not* squinting, even though the summer sun is so bright. I look very happy. I *am* very happy.

"Thank you, Ben," I say into the phone. "How do I print this photo?"

He explains over the phone, and soon I've got the picture in my hand. I take a thumbtack and stick it to the wall near my bed. After a relaxing shower, I shuffle into my room wearing my favorite fluffy robe.

I see myself with my son and my granddaughter smiling happily in the park. Next time, I think, I will have a picture with my daughter-in-law too. Sarah is coming home tomorrow. Maybe this weekend we can go to the park again!

I snuggle into the soft sheets of my bed. I managed to escape without any sunburn, but my eyes are tired from the bright summer day.

There were several bits of grass stuck in my hair when I washed it earlier. I also found a few breadcrumbs leftover in my pocket from feeding the geese.

I turn off my lamp and lie awake in the darkness.

Today was a perfect day in the park. Outside, the summer storm drums against my roof. But the weather forecast promises that tomorrow will be sunny, too. If it's not too hot, I'll walk to Ben and Sarah's.

The carnations are blooming in my garden. I could cut a few to give to Sarah. She's a lovely girl.

I fall asleep slowly, smiling when I think about my family. I can't wait to go with them to the park again. When I dream, all four of us are in the park. The red-haired lady is singing. Ben and Sarah dance. Hannah and I sit with the park bench cat. The sun is shining in the summer-blue sky. We each have our favorite flavor of ice cream.

Yes. A summer day spent in the park is my dream come true.

Printed in Great Britain
by Amazon